Raggedy Ann
and the COOKIE SNATCHER

by Barbara Shook Hazen

illustrated by June Goldsborough

GOLDEN PRESS
Western Publishing Company, Inc.
Racine, Wisconsin

Tenth Printing, 1981
Copyright © 1972 by The Bobbs-Merrill Company, Inc. Printed in the U.S.A. by Western Publishing Company, Inc. All rights reserved. No part of this book may be reproduced or copied in any form without written permission from the publisher. GOLDEN®, A LITTLE GOLDEN BOOK®, and GOLDEN PRESS® are trademarks of Western Publishing Company, Inc.

Raggedy Ann loved to do things for Raggedy Andy and the other dolls. Most of all, she enjoyed cooking for them. Today, as a special treat, she was baking sugar cookies.

Everyone helped. As Raggedy Ann read the recipe aloud, Soldier Doll broke the eggs, China Doll sifted the flour, and Andy waited to beat the batter.

"Yum-yum," said Andy. He licked a bit of batter off his hand. "These cookies are going to be delicious. I could eat them all."

"Not yet," said Raggedy Ann. "First we must cut them out. What shape shall we make them?"

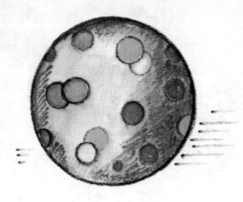

"Round, like my ball," said Andy.

"Square, like my blocks," said Soldier Doll.

"A triangle, like my tepee," said Indian Doll.

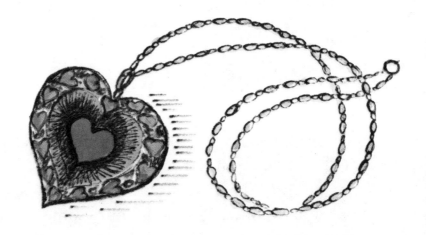

"Heart-shaped, like my locket," pleaded China Doll. "Oh, please, Raggedy Ann."

"I know what we'll do," said Raggedy Ann. "We'll cut out some of each shape."

So she did. She cut out some round cookies and some square ones. She cut out some that were triangle-shaped and some that were heart-shaped. Then she placed the cookies on a cookie sheet and slid them into the oven.

Soldier Doll timed the cookies while they were in the oven, to make sure they didn't burn.

Toot, toot, toot! He blew his bugle three times when the cookies were done.

Everyone crowded around Raggedy Ann.

"May I have one—just one?" they all asked.

"Not yet," said Raggedy Ann firmly. "The cookies have to cool before we can eat them." So she took them out to the porch and left them there to cool.

When Raggedy Ann went back for her cookies, *they were gone!* She could hardly believe her shoe-button eyes. Every single cookie was gone! Someone was a cookie snatcher, but who could it be?

The only clue was a set of muddy footprints going up the porch steps to the cookie sheet.

"Andy! Dolls! Come quickly!" Raggedy Ann called. "Someone has taken all the cookies. Someone is a cookie snatcher!"

She thought a minute, then remembered how Raggedy Andy had said he could eat all of the cookies.

"Tell me the truth, Andy," Raggedy Ann begged. "Did you take the cookies?"

"Cross my heart, I didn't," said Andy. "I'm not a cookie snatcher."

"Neither are we," said all the other dolls.

There was only one friend who could help. Raggedy Ann raced across the yard to see him.

His name was Peterkins, and he lived next door. Peterkins was a hound dog with a supersensitive nose. He could sniff out anything, anytime.

"I'm glad you're home," said Raggedy Ann. "Oh, Peterkins, you must help me. I want you to do something very big and very important."

Peterkins rolled his eyes. He tried to imagine what the big, important job might be.

Did Raggedy Ann want him to help the school-children across the street? That would be a big, important thing to do.

Or maybe she wanted him to guard a treasure she had found. That would be a good job for a brave hound dog like himself.

Perhaps Raggedy Ann wanted him to ride on the big red fire engine with the firemen. What a fine job that would be!

Then Raggedy Ann told him what had happened. "Oh, Peterkins, only you can help me. Someone took all the cookies I baked for Andy and the dolls. Your super nose can sniff out the cookie snatcher." Raggedy Ann began to cry. "The only clue I have is a set of muddy footprints just like—"

"Just like the ones near my doghouse," said Peterkins sadly. He hung his head and moaned. "I did it," he said. "I'm the cookie snatcher, but I couldn't help it. Those cookies smelled so good, and no one has ever baked anything for me."

Raggedy Ann put her arms around Peterkins. "That is too bad," she said. "And it must have been hard for you to tell the truth. But I'm very glad you did." Then she said, "Now, you wait here, and I'll be back with a surprise."

Cookies

And what do you think she did then? First she baked a new batch of cookies for Raggedy Andy, Soldier Doll, Indian Doll, and China Doll. Then she baked a special cake just for Peterkins.

"Surprise!" said Raggedy Ann. "And it's all for you, because you were brave and told the truth."

Peterkins sniffed his cake happily. "Thank you," he said. "I'm a very lucky hound dog. And I like the shape of this cake, Raggedy Ann."

The surprise cake for Peterkins wasn't a circle or a square. It wasn't a triangle, and it wasn't heart-shaped. It was a special cake—in the shape of a doghouse!—and the name on the roof was PETERKINS.